TO THE MOUNTAINS
BY MORNING

For Mrs. P. — D.W.
For my parents, Ping and Haoyin — A.Z.

Groundwood Books / Douglas & McIntyre Ltd.
585 Bloor Street West
Toronto, Ontario M6G 1K5

The publisher gratefully acknowledges the assistance of the Canada Council, the Ontario Arts Council and the Ontario Ministry of Culture, Tourism and Recreation.

Canadian Cataloguing in Publication

Wieler, Diana J. (Diana Jean), 1961-
To the mountains by morning

ISBN 0-88899-227-0

I. Zhang, Ange. II. Title.

PS8595.I53143T6 1995   jC813'.54   C95-931021-5
PZ7.W54To 1995

First published in the United States in 1996
The illustrations are done in acrylics.
Design by Michael Solomon
Printed and bound in Hong Kong by Everbest Printing Co. Ltd.

TO THE MOUNTAINS BY MORNING

DIANA WIELER

ILLUSTRATED BY

ANGE ZHANG

A GROUNDWOOD BOOK

DOUGLAS & McINTYRE ✱ VANCOUVER / TORONTO

THE Rocky Mountain Stables lay in the foothills, just beyond the edge of the prairie. At the stables, children and grown-ups rented horses for trail rides. One of the best horses for riding was Old Bailey, a strong chestnut quarter horse. Her large wide hooves kept her steady on any trail, and her strong back could carry the heaviest person.

Old Bailey had seen ten summers at the Rocky Mountain Stables, and in all those years, she had grown smart. She knew who would treat her gently, and who would kick her sides or pull her reins too tightly. She could tell just by looking at people.

One day Old Bailey saw a little boy scamper up onto her friend Dreamy Day's back.

"Watch out for that one," Old Bailey warned. "He thinks he's a real cowboy."

Sure enough, the little boy dug his heels in so hard that Dreamy Day snorted in hurt surprise. Old Bailey tossed her head sadly. She hated to be right about people, but she always was.

All the horses at the stable admired Old Bailey and looked up to her. Well, *almost* all of them. No one really knew why Stocking disliked Old Bailey so much. Stocking had come to the Rocky Mountain Stables about two years ago, and he was surely the most striking horse in the barn. His coat was a beautiful shining black, with a white blaze on his forehead and a white foreleg on the right side. Old Bailey had been as kind to him as she was to every new horse, but he never returned the courtesy.

"Ah, Old Bailey doesn't know so much," Stocking used to say. "She's nothing but an old bag of bones."

Old Bailey would just stare back at him.

"Hard workers last longer than beauty queens," was Old Bailey's answer, and no one could prove her wrong. In her ten years she had seen sixteen horses come and go.

The horses came from all over the country, with frightened eyes and nervous feet. They came not knowing what they were supposed to do or what was going to happen to them. Sometimes the regulars like Stocking gave a new horse the cold shoulder, but Old Bailey never did.

"I *like* to make new friends," she explained, and then she would go out of her way to teach the newcomers the ropes.

She'd show them all the tricks and all the trails, but some of the new horses just weren't good with people. They couldn't get used to all the different types who rode on their backs and kicked at their sides. Then the day would come when they'd flare up and throw a rider.

"It's only natural," said the other horses sympathetically.

"It's bad for business," the owners said, and the new horse would go. Nobody knew where.

Those were the saddest mornings, when the new horses were taken away. Right after breakfast the horse trailer would pull up to the barns and a stable hand would grab the new-comer's halter.

"Bailey, Bailey! Where are they taking me?" the frightened horse would call.

"To a better place, dear," Old Bailey would breathe softly, but of course she didn't know.

When the trailer was loaded and out of sight, the others huddled together and stared with large, silent eyes.

"I'm sure they're being sold to other stables," Mad Dancer said once, as brightly as he could.

The horses nodded to each other because they really wanted to believe that. Stocking spat on the ground.

"The *young* ones are sold to other stables," he said smugly, and everyone knew what he meant. *Old* horses were cheaply bought and cheaply sold.

"I've heard terrible stories," Dreamy Day whispered, "about horses being sold for dog food."

"Don't be silly," Old Bailey comforted. "That's cruel! They don't do that any more." Seven pairs of wide eyes stared back at her silently. The horses hoped she was right.

That was how the horses lived. Days at the Rocky Mountain Stables passed easily with a few trail rides. The barn was warm at night, and meals were regular and filling. From the yard where they spent their mornings, the horses could see the beautiful mountains, and they did their very best not to think about the day when the horse trailer might come for them. They succeeded well, up until Mr. Cuthbert came.

Mr. Cuthbert was the fourth owner of the stables. He wore funny green pants that came only to his knees, and he carried a riding crop under his arm. The horses could tell he was different right from the start. On the day he bought the stables, he walked around the grounds, staring and staring at everything he saw.

"It's all so dingy!" he exclaimed to Joe, one of the stable hands. "Why is that?"

"Well, I dunno," Joe shrugged. All the riding stables *he* knew looked just like this one.

Mr. Cuthbert strode into the barn where the horses lived, and suddenly staggered backwards, holding his nose.

"What a smell!" the new owner wheezed. "Why on earth is that?"

"Well, I dunno," Joe said again, scratching his head. All the riding stables *he* knew smelled just like this one.

Mr. Cuthbert ran his hand over his short silver hair. "Bring the horses out one at a time. I want to see what I've gotten myself into."

One after another the horses were led into the bright sunshine. It soon became clear that Mr. Cuthbert had never owned a riding stable before. He looked at the horses' feet instead of their teeth to see how old they were. He hung onto their tails to keep them still. All the while he was grading them.

"How straggly! That horse's tail hasn't been combed!"

"So scruffy! This one has knobby knees!"

When Joe led Old Bailey out into the yard, Mr. Cuthbert gasped.

"Good heavens, what an old nag! What do you call this one?"

The stable hand slapped Old Bailey's broad haunches proudly. "This one here? She's Old Bailey and gentle as a kitten. She's been with us ten years, and she ain't never thrown a rider yet."

Mr. Cuthbert was shaking his head. "Enough, enough! I don't want to see any more!" He turned and faced the yard. "There are going to be big changes here, I promise you. I'm going to turn this business right around. In two weeks' time you won't even recognize the place!"

Joe yawned and scratched his stomach.

Mr. Cuthbert was certainly a man of his word. In only a week's time the Rocky Mountain Stables was completely different. In fact, no one had ever seen anything like it!

Mr. Cuthbert's first official act was to paint everything yellow. The house and the stables were all done over with two coats of the brightest, yellowest paint the store could supply. Even the rocks in the driveway were painted yellow.

The horses thought it looked awful and smelled worse. They walked around the yard wrinkling their noses and looking for fresh air. But there was nowhere they could be free of the horrible yellow paint. Dreamy Day stepped in a whole bucketful, and Mad Dancer got some on his tail and swished it against Old Bailey's backside.

"It'll come to no good," Old Bailey muttered, and the others perked up their ears. Old Bailey had been especially quiet lately, and the horses were suddenly anxious to know what she thought.

"What do you mean?" Dreamy Day asked.

The old horse sighed. "Just look around you, at all the changes. I've got a feeling about Mr. Green Pants, and I've got it bad."

The others stood silently. They knew that Old Bailey was never wrong about people, and that made them quiver in their stomachs. Slowly the chestnut horse turned and plodded away to stand alone by the fence. She knew her time was coming.

More changes followed the yellow paint. A flashy new sign was put up at the entrance to the stables. Then Mr. Cuthbert took a long hard look at the yard where the horses spent their mornings.

"Awfully low fence, don't you think?" he asked Joe.

The stable hand sighed. He had learned that Mr. Cuthbert's questions usually meant more work for *him*.

The new owner tapped one of the posts with his riding crop. "Why, a horse could clear that fence with no trouble and be off and gone before we knew."

"Oh, they'd never do that," Joe said.

"Why not?" Mr. Cuthbert asked.

The stable hand pointed to his head. "They're smart; they got horse sense. They know there's nowhere for 'em to go." He swept his arm across the horizon. "There's nothing to eat out there except brush and bramble, and no nice warm barn to sleep in. Besides, unless they could make it to the mountains by morning, we'd round 'em up pretty quick. I told ya, they got horse sense."

Mr. Cuthbert wasn't impressed. "Well, I have new horses coming in, and I want to protect my investment. We'll build a fence so high and so strong a bulldozer couldn't knock it down!"

Word of the new fence and the new horses spread quickly. In horror the regulars watched their familiar yard being torn apart by roaring machines that belched black smoke. Deep holes were dug, and posts the size of tree trunks were cemented in.

Dreamy Day was frightened by the noise, and she stayed close to Old Bailey.

"Oh, Bailey," she moaned, "what's happening? What will become of us?"

Old Bailey swallowed and tried to show a cheerfulness she didn't feel. "Oh, you'll have nothing to worry about, dear. You're a beautiful bay horse, and young, too! You'll stay on here for years and years."

Across the barn, Stocking's sharp ears perked up. Smiling smugly, he trotted over.

"Of course she'll stay," he said. "They'll keep any horse *worth* anything. It's the others who have to worry."

"Just what do you mean?" Dreamy Day asked sharply.

Stocking narrowed his eyes. "There are eight of us, and eight more to come. How many stalls do you count in the barn?"

Sandy, a strawberry roan, looked left and right.

"Fifteen," he said.

"Any way you add it up, it's one stall short," Stocking smiled, looking at Bailey. "And all your wisdom and fine words won't save you then."

The others whirled to look at Bailey, and she stared back with eyes that had seen ten summers and a heart that knew people better than they knew themselves. She didn't have to say anything. Out in the yard the machines roared and roared.

WHEN Stocking awoke in the middle of the night, he felt that something was wrong. The barn door hung wide open, and the moon shone brightly on the stable floor. But listening carefully to the deep and measured breathing around him, Stocking prepared to settle back down to sleep. Then, through a knothole in his stall, he saw one gleaming eye. It was Old Bailey's. She was wide awake in the stall next to him. Thinking of the day's conversation, Stocking didn't want to miss a chance to rub salt in the wound.

"Calm night, Bailey," he said curtly.

"Beautiful," she whispered. "As beautiful as the night I first came here."

"You remember back *that* far?" Stocking laughed with a snort.

"Of course I do," she breathed, and she shifted her weight. "I was only a yearling, and nervous as anything. I'd never been away from my mother, and I couldn't sleep. It was a night as calm and beautiful as this."

"So you're just staying awake, thinking about the good old days?" Stocking teased. Old Bailey swished her tail sharply.

"Come now, Stocking," she said softly. "We've known each other a long time. Let's not play games any more."

Stocking snorted in surprise and opened his mouth to say something, but Old Bailey cut him off.

"We both know who's going to make room for that extra horse," she continued. "The stable owners always send away old horses. I've lived a long time, and I knew this day would come. I just didn't know I'd be so...so...frightened."

For once Stocking was at a loss. He wanted to shoot back a quick retort, but all the angry, bitter words were suddenly melting inside him.

"M-m-maybe you'll go to another farm," he managed to say at last, but the chestnut horse stamped her foot impatiently.

"I'm ten years old," she sighed. "There will be no other farm. The horse trailer is coming for me the day after tomorrow. I've heard them talking."

Old Bailey sighed again and turned her head away to sleep. But sleep didn't come to the horse beside her. Stocking could see it all clearly in his mind now, a picture he couldn't turn away from. He could see the horse trailer backing up to the barn and Joe the stable hand taking hold of Bailey's halter. Then he pictured the day when the trailer would come for him.

"That's many years away," he whispered to himself. "Horses live a long time."

"But not forever," his thoughts rang back. A beautiful black coat would one day be ratty and gray. The strongest back would eventually break. Stocking knew the deep night and then the dawn.

THE new fence was finished by noon. It led directly off the stable so that the horses couldn't leave the barn without going to their new yard. High, heavy posts were cemented into the ground while others lay horizontally, with only enough space between them for the horses to poke their noses through.

"Now *there's* a fence for you!" Mr. Cuthbert called proudly.

"It's like a prison!" Stocking thought frantically. He and the others galloped from one end to the other, whinnying. The only one who was quiet was Old Bailey.

She plodded up and down the length of the fence, like a tiger in a cage. She sniffed it and then continued walking, up and down.

The sight of her made Mr. Cuthbert think.

"Let's go back to the house, Joe," he said to the stable hand, "and finish up that bit of...uh, business." If Old Bailey shivered slightly, no one saw it. She continued walking, up and down.

That night Stocking had a dream. He dreamed of something he'd seen once—a little girl on a swing. She started off barely rocking, but by pumping her legs and pulling back with her arms, she rose higher and higher. Suddenly, when the swing was at its highest, the little girl let go with a cry of delight and went sailing through the air!

The dark horse was jolted awake, the dream-picture strong in his mind. He quickly turned to the stable on his left, and he knew he really hadn't been dreaming. Old Bailey's stall was empty.

A wooden bar lay across the front of each stall, but like every other horse, Stocking knew how to lift it. He pushed up under the bar with his strong nose, and it swung back easily. Stocking trotted into the yard.

THE moon was high over the Rocky Mountain Stables, and the yard was lit with a silver sheen. When Old Bailey heard Stocking's quiet hoofbeats, she turned and waited.

The two horses stared at each other for a long time.

"You're trying to escape," Stocking said at last.

"Yes," Old Bailey replied evenly.

"You might break a leg, Bailey," Stocking warned. "It's a high fence."

"I have to take that chance. It's better than just waiting for the trailer," the old horse said.

"You know, I could kick up a fuss right now, and Mr. Green Pants would be here in a minute."

"I know," Old Bailey answered.

"But I won't," Stocking said. "I'm coming with you."

The old horse caught her breath in astonishment. Not in ten summers, not in a hundred, would she have imagined him saying that. Her eyes narrowed, studying him.

"It's a hard road," Old Bailey stated flatly. "If we get over the fence, we have to run without stopping. We have to make it to the mountains by morning. Even then we'll be in danger for the rest of our lives."

"I know," Stocking said. "I'm coming with you."

At last Old Bailey smiled. "Then let's go!" She swung around and trotted to the far end of the yard. She flew towards the fence. With a magnificent push she sailed through the air, just like the girl on the swing in Stocking's dream.

As soon as Old Bailey cleared the fence, Stocking galloped around the yard, building up speed. On the second time around he leaped with all the strength and muscle that a desperate young horse can possess. He landed, gasping, on the other side.

"To the mountains!" Old Bailey cried, tossing her head.

"By morning," Stocking breathed, and in a rush of midnight wind they were off, thundering over the foothills.